Lrep

For Seth, Jane, and Rob, with thanks for speaking
— E. C. K.

For Tiffany
— J. K.

Text copyright © 2003 by Elizabeth Cody Kimmel
Illustrations copyright © 2003 by Joung Un Kim

First edition 2003

Library of Congress Cataloging-in-Publication Data
Kimmel, Elizabeth Cody.
What do you dream? / Elizabeth Cody Kimmel ; illustrated by Joung Un Kim. — 1st ed.
Summary: Presents a circle of dreams that leads from a child to a flower to a butterfly and
eventually up to the moon and back to the earth, which is dreaming of a child.
ISBN 0-7636-1338-X
[1. Nature — Fiction. 2. Dreams — Fiction.] I. Kim, Joung Un, ill. II. Title.
PZ7.K56475 Wh 2003
[E] — dc21   2002067661

2 4 6 8 10 9 7 5 3 1

Printed in China

This book was typeset in Sanvito Light.
The illustrations were done in acrylic.

Candlewick Press
2067 Massachusetts Avenue
Cambridge, Massachusetts 02140

visit us at www.candlewick.com

What Do You Dream?

Elizabeth Cody Kimmel

illustrated by Joung Un Kim

CANDLEWICK PRESS
CAMBRIDGE, MASSACHUSETTS

Child, tell me,
of what do you dream?

I dream of a flower
in a sweet green meadow.

Flower, tell me,
of what do you dream?

I dream of a butterfly
with petal-soft wings.

Butterfly, tell me,
of what do you dream?

I dream of a tree
hugging sky in its branches.

Tree, tell me,
of what do you dream?

I dream of the wind
and its gentle cool kisses.

Wind, tell me,
of what do you dream?

I dream of a cloud
as it billows and hovers.

Cloud, tell me,
of what do you dream?

I dream of rain
tickling the ground with soft drops.

Rain, tell me,
of what do you dream?

I dream of the sun
and its warm golden fingers.

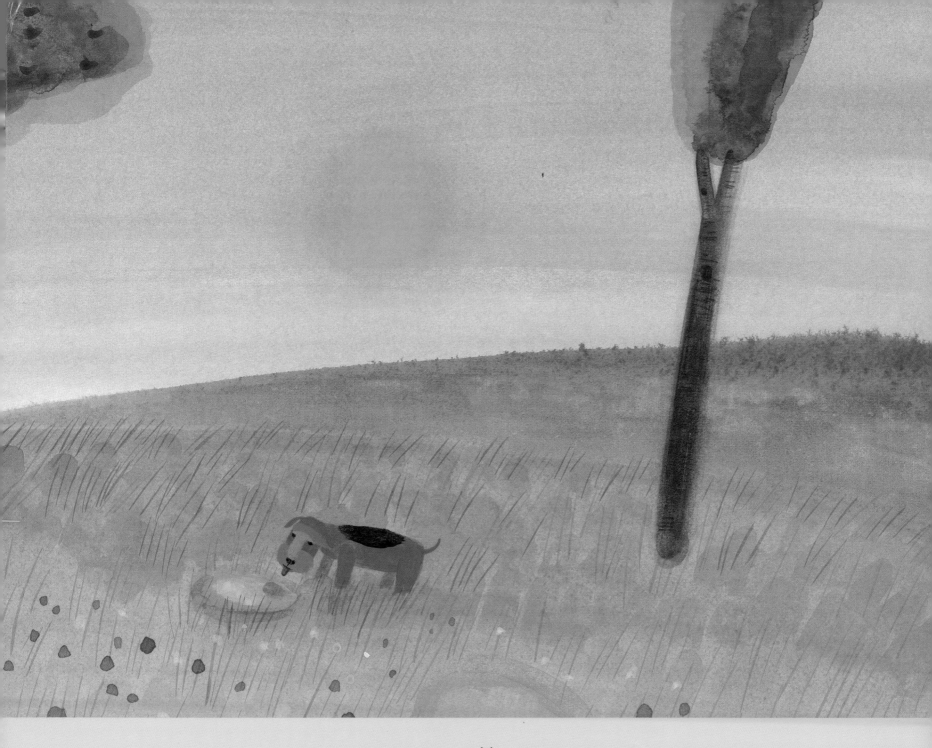

Sun, tell me,
of what do you dream?

I dream of the moon
smiling bright through the night.

Moon, tell me,
of what do you dream?

I dream of the Earth
humming gently with life.

Earth, tell me,
of what do you dream?

I dream of a child . . .

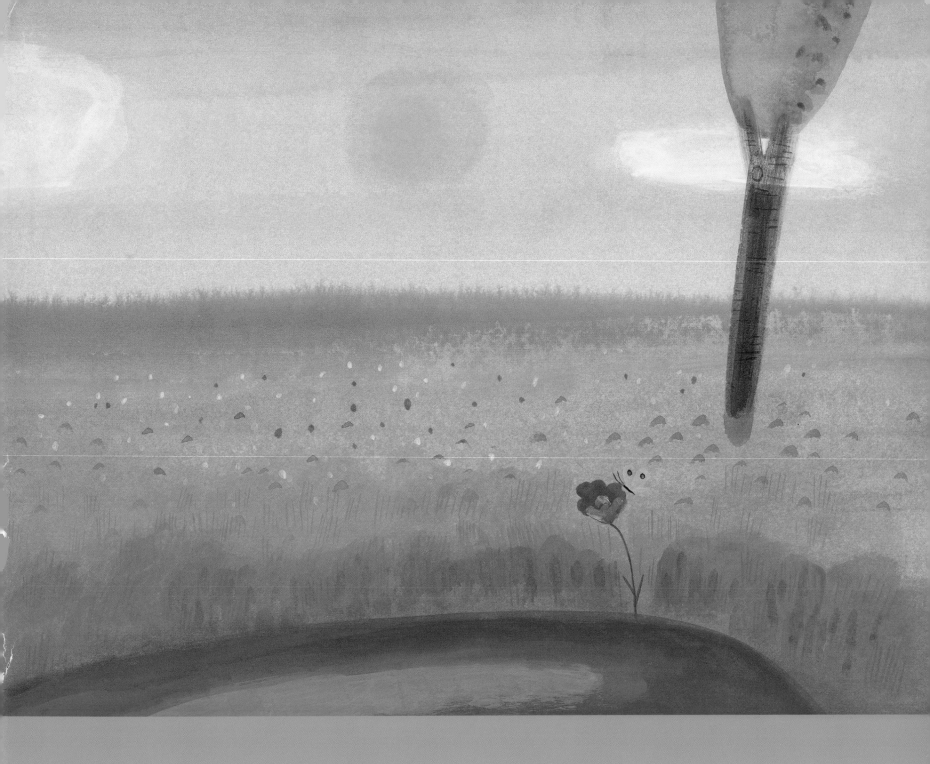

. . . dreaming of me.